Stick & FETCH INVESTIGATE

A girl. A dog. A detective agency.

For Martin, Lord Roxbee of Bexhill, after whom
the hotel was named P.A.

For Noah – who reminds me of Tofu – and his humans,
Sam and Nick E.E.

This is a work of fiction. Names, characters, places and incidents are either
the product of the author's imagination or, if real, are used fictitiously.

First published 2020 by Walker Books Ltd
87 Vauxhall Walk, London SE11 5HJ

10 9 8 7 6 5 4 3 2 1

Text © 2020 Philip Ardagh
Illustrations © 2020 Elissa Elwick

The right of Philip Ardagh and Elissa Elwick to be identified as author
and illustrator respectively of this work has been asserted by them in accordance
with the Copyright, Designs and Patents Act 1988

This book has been typeset in Anke Sans

Printed and bound in China

British Library Cataloguing in Publication Data: a catalogue
record for this book is available from the British Library

ISBN 978-1-4063-9239-5

www.walker.co.uk

Stick & FETCH INVESTIGATE

OFF THE LEASH

IN
THEIR FIRST FULL-LENGTH ADVENTURE

Philip Ardagh

illustrated by

Elissa Elwick

WALKER
BOOKS

CONTENTS

CHAPTER 1

THE SCENE OF THE CRIME......11

CHAPTER 2

CAUSE FOR ALARM......41

CHAPTER 3

CAT!!!......59

CHAPTER 4

AN UNINVITED VISITOR......79

CHAPTER 5

CAPTAIN BOFF......103

✴

CHAPTER 6

JUSTICE AT LAST!......127

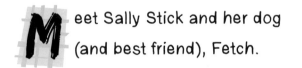

Meet Sally Stick and her dog (and best friend), Fetch.

Together, they're:

STICK & FETCH, DETECTIVES.

Like most top **DETECTIVES**, Stick and Fetch are never fully off duty.

They may look as if they're playing in the park, or watching telly, or reading a book ... but they always have an eye out for the next case to **solve**.

They may seem like an ordinary girl with her ordinary (lovable) dog … but don't be fooled! When it comes to solving *mysteries* so mysterious that most people don't even think they ARE *mysteries*, STICK & FETCH are Number One.

Ready with her **DETECTIVE** notebook, pencil and magnifying glass, Sally Stick is on the case! Ready with a doggy nose for sniffing out **CLUES** and doggy ears that can hear the frying of a sausage two houses away, Fetch is at her side.

The office of **STICK & FETCH, DETECTIVES** is usually to be found in Granny Stick's kitchen, in the house where the three of them live.

But not this time.

This time, it's located in Room 402 of *The Roxbee Hotel*...

The Roxbee Hotel
Number One for Pets & People

★ Perfect for piranhas!   ★ Brilliant for budgies!
★ A delight for dogs!   ★ Super for snakes!
★ Fabulous for fishes!   ★ Cozy for cats!

"We came for a night and stayed for a year!"
Mr Van Winkle

CHAPTER 1

THE SCENE OF THE CRIME

**G**ranny Stick and Sally Stick were going on holiday – which meant, of course, that Fetch was going on holiday too. Stick and Fetch are **DETECTIVE** partners so they go everywhere together, just in case there's a case to be **solved** (and because they love each other).

They were going to stay in a hotel. Granny Stick had recently had an operation in hospital, and — although she was much, much better now — she needed a break from cooking and clearing up after two, very busy, **DETECTIVES**.

Sally had been reading a leaflet about the hotel and was very excited. "There's a lounge and a library and a games room and a restaurant and a juice bar and—"

WOOF! said Fetch excitedly.

Sally had already told him this a **GAZILLION** times, but she was telling him again because they'd never stayed in a hotel before.

"It's pet-friendly, so you can be off the leash as long as you behave yourself," said Sally as they walked up the steps to the front door.

"You can go here, there and everywhere, Fetch," she explained. "Except for other people's rooms, the restaurant and, of course, the kitchen."

WOOF! woofed Fetch. He was hoping that pet-friendly didn't mean cat-friendly!

The
~~Pet-Friendly~~ Hotel
BUT NO CATS!

★ ★ ★

xbee H
Number One for Pets

He gave a shudder that made his hair fluff out. Fetch HATES cats. His worst enemy

in the whole wide world is a Persian cat
called Tofu.

Tofu was one of the reasons Fetch
was looking forward to the holiday so
much. Well, getting *away* from Tofu.
Fetch is sure Tofu deliberately prowls the
neighbourhood, just to upset him!

Inside, they found themselves in a large entrance hall.

"Good afternoon!" said a cheery man behind the reception desk. "Welcome to *The Roxbee Hotel*."

"Thank you," said Granny Stick. "We're the Sticks. We're here for the week."

Sally had never stayed in a hotel before, and it felt very exciting to be staying a whole WEEK.

The man, whose gold name badge said WINSTON, tapped something into a computer and looked at the screen.

"Welcome, Mrs Stick. You're in Room 402. It has a lovely view. Morris will show you to your room." With that he dinged a bell on the counter and a smartly dressed young man appeared. "Please show these ladies to 402, Morris," he said.

Ladies? Sally liked the idea of being a lady (though she liked the idea of being a **DETECTIVE** even more).

The young man took Granny Stick's suitcase in his left hand and tucked Sally's smaller suitcase under his left arm, leaving his right hand free to press a button in the wall. Two doors slid open.

Granny Stick stepped inside, followed by Sally with the dog basket, followed by Fetch wagging his tail. Then Morris joined them and pressed a button marked "4". The doors closed. It was a bit of a squeeze.

Fetch was puzzled. To be honest, he was disappointed. The room was tiny!

Then there was a rumbling sound and the floor vibrated.

WOOF? he barked.

"Nothing to worry about," said Sally. "It's only the lift taking us up to the fourth floor."

Fetch was very relieved. Of course, he'd been in lifts before, but never one this rickety, or with padded velvet walls!

Room 402 was fantastic. It was really two rooms. Three, if you counted the bathroom, which Sally did. Twice. There was Granny Stick's room with a nice big double bed and a bay window, and two more doors. One opened on to the bathroom, which had a bath and a separate shower cubicle.

On a glass shelf above the basin,
there was a neat row of little silver-topped
plastic bottles of shampoo, bubble bath,
shower gel and hand lotion. And a tiny
soap sealed in a packet.

Fetch put his front paws up on the
rim of the basin and gave the soap a
sniff. "That's hardly big enough to wash
my paws with!" he said. All Granny Stick
heard, of course, was, **WOOF!**

"And what a waste of plastic!" said Sally. "They'll probably end up in the ocean upsetting turtles."

Fetch tried to imagine turtles using shampoo. *But they don't have hair*, he thought.

The last door opened on to another, smaller bedroom with a single bed and a little round window.

"We've got our very own room!" said Sally. "It's got a porthole, like in a ship!" She lifted Fetch up so that he could look out of it with her.

"I can see the sea!" said Fetch. **WOOF!**

"You're right!" said Sally. There was
a sparkling patch of blue sea just beyond
the treetops.

Sally looked around. There was a small
table up against the opposite wall. On it

was a lamp and some smart notepaper with *The Roxbee Hotel* printed at the top. "This will make a very good office for the **DETECTIVE** agency," she told her **DETECTIVE** partner.

She quickly unpacked her bag and put Scruff, her most important teddy, on her pillow. Fetch took Squeaky  Duck, *his* most special toy, in his mouth. It squeaked reassuringly as he carefully hid it under the bed.

They bounded back into Granny's
room. "Can we explore now?" asked Sally.

Granny was putting her clothes into a
chest of drawers. "Yes," she said. "As long
as you stay inside, don't go into anyone's
room and DON'T DISTURB ANYBODY!"

"We won't!" said Sally Stick.

"As if we'd do that," said Fetch indignantly. **WOOF!**

"Good," said Granny Stick. "Right, I think I'll have a little nap after our journey."

STICK & FETCH closed the door quietly behind them, and walked down the fourth-floor corridor, back towards the lift. The carpet was covered in orange whorls. It made Fetch feel a bit woozy just looking at them ...

... which may be why he walked –
SLAP! BANG! – into a trolley.

"Oof!" said Fetch. The bottom shelf of
the trolley was piled high with fluffy towels
and his nose had ended up in one of them.

He was a little embarrassed that he
hadn't been looking where he was going.
But what a silly place to leave a trolley!

Sally Stick bent down and scooped Fetch up in her arms. This isn't standard **procedure** for *DETECTIVE* partners, but it was an easy way to let him see the top of the trolley.

It was divided into compartments for the different types of bottles, just like the ones in their bathroom.

"Hmmm," said Sally Stick.

"Hmmm," said her **DETECTIVE** partner.

"Are you thinking what I'm thinking?" asked Sally.

"What ARE you thinking?" asked Fetch.

"I'm thinking that this is a **GETAWAY**

TROLLEY!" said Sally. "You couldn't fit a **GETAWAY CAR** in this corridor so a trolley had to do."

"Getting away from what?" asked Fetch, back on the floor now, tongue lolling in excitement.

"The *CRIME*," said Sally. "Someone has been breaking into the rooms, *STEALING* little bottles of shampoo and towels. See!" She pointed at the bottom shelf. "They've

only **STOLEN** the nice clean ones!"

Fetch looked up and down the hotel corridor. "But where are the **thieves** now?" he asked.

"Hiding, of course!" said Sally. "They must have found out that two top **DETECTIVES** are staying in Room 402, and they fled the scene when they heard our door opening!"

"Then I'll sniff them out, the rotten

thieves!" Fetch declared, and he charged off down the corridor with Sally in hot pursuit.

Rounding the corner, Fetch skidded to a halt, only JUST managing not to trip over his ears. There, in front of them, was a woman. She was lying face down on the carpet.

STICK & FETCH had solved lots of CRIMES before but never one involving a BODY! Well, not one lying on the floor, anyway. And in a hotel corridor, no less. They had been searching for shampoo thieves but had discovered …

"A victim!" said Sally. She gasped.

"A what?" asked Fetch. WOOF?

"A **victim**," said Sally. "A **victim** is someone who's had a **CRIME** done to them. We need to search the area for evidence."

Next to the woman was a big plastic bottle. Fetch sniffed it. **POISON!** he woofed.

CHAPTER 2

CAUSE FOR ALARM

YELP!

ithout warning, the **victim** moved!

Fetch yelped: **YELP!**

Sally nearly jumped out of her skin. (Not really, but that's what it felt like.) "You're alive!" she spluttered as the woman got into a kneeling position. Sally was ever-so-slightly disappointed.

"I not see you there!" said the woman

in surprise. Her gold name badge read
SOFIA. She pointed down at the floor.
"Stain. Bad stain," she said.

Both Sally and Fetch looked.

"*BLOOD?*" asked Sally.

Fetch sniffed the stain. "Tomato ketchup," he announced. *WOOF!*

"Good work, partner," said Stick. She saw that Sofia had been attacking the stain with a cloth soaked in liquid poured from the bottle.

I think she needs glasses, thought Sally. *Strong ones!*

Sofia bent down and patted Fetch on the head. "Nice doggie," she said.

Fetch looked up proudly and frantically wagged his tail. "I like her," he told Sally.

"So do I!" said Sally.

Stick and Fetch ALWAYS like it when people say *nice* things about Fetch.

"We're **DETECTIVES**," said Sally, pulling out one of her STICK & FETCH business cards from the top pocket of her dress. She handed it to the woman.

Sofia took the card and studied it
closely. It was blank.

She turned it over.
It was blank on
that side, too.
"**DETECTIFF?**"
she asked.
"Yes," said Sally.
"My partner and I are on the **trail**
of some hotel **thieves**."

"We just found their abandoned GETAWAY TROLLEY," said Fetch.

All Sofia heard, of course, was, *WOOF! WOOF!*

"Is blank," she said, holding up the card.

"No time to explain!" said Sally Stick. "We have **thieves** to catch. Bye!"

A quick look around the fourth floor revealed that no one was lurking in the corridor. Stick LOVED bounding up and down. He'd never been in a building with so much s-p-a-c-e!

Sally found a walk-in cupboard and they checked it out for hidden shampoo.

All they found was:

a mop and bucket

a dustpan and brush

bin liners (small, white)

bin liners (black, large)

three pairs of yellow rubber gloves
(medium)

Sally wrote all these down in her
DETECTIVE notebook with her **DETECTIVE**
pencil.

"Anything else?" Sally asked Fetch, who was giving the walk-in cupboard one final sniff.

"Yes!" he said. "Chocolate!" Using his nose, he nudged a chocolate-wrapper out from behind the bucket.

BANDIT

"Excellent work, **DETECTIVE**!" said Stick. She picked up the wrapper. It had the word BANDIT written on it. "Wow!" she said. "You know what a BANDIT is, don't you, Fetch?"

WOOF? asked Fetch.

"A BANDIT is a **baddy**! A **thief**! This must be a special type of chocolate bar for **baddies**!" Sally Stick sucked the end of her pencil. "Here's what I think happened...

"The **thief** was breaking into rooms, *STEALING* shampoo and towels and things and putting them on the **GETAWAY TROLLEY** when they heard us coming out

of our room. They panicked, abandoned the trolley and hid from us in this cupboard."

"Eating chocolate," Fetch added.

"Yup," said Stick. "Then they slipped away while we were talking to Sofia and **investigating** the carpet stain."

"Which means they can't have gone far!" said Fetch.

"You're right!" said Sally. "I haven't heard the lift ping. Let's check the stairs."

Beside the lift there was a door with a notice on it.

Sally Stick read the notice out to Fetch. He reads very well for a dog but finds some long words quite tricky.

"What does 'alarmed' mean?" he asked.

"Frightened," said Sally. "'Don't be alarmed' means 'Don't be frightened'."

How can a door be frightened? Fetch wondered. *Maybe it doesn't like being an emergency door.*

"We need to find these BANDITS who are *STEALING* from the rooms," declared Sally. "That's definitely an emergency!"

WOOF! said Fetch.

"So let's go!" said Sally, pushing open the door.

An alarm started to wail LOUDLY.

CHAPTER 3

CAT!!!

I t was easier for Stick to run down the stairs than it was for Fetch, as she has longer legs. (Even if he does have four and she only has two.) They'd passed two floors when they ran slam-bam into someone coming the other way.

"oOOF!"
AROOOOOOOH!

The **AROOOOOOOH**! came from Fetch. All seven "o"s of it. In the kerfuffle, Sally had trodden on his tail. She scooped him up and kissed his nose.

"I'm SO sorry, Fetch," she said. Then she turned to the person they'd run into. "Look what you made me go and do!" she said crossly.

A woman with a very tall, wobbly hairdo stared at them both, as the alarm continued to sound. "Are you all right?" she asked. "What's the emergency?"

Her gold name badge read CLAIRE and underneath were written the words **_GENERAL MANAGER_**.

"We're on the trail of some shampoo-and-clean-towel **thieves**, General," said Sally. "We think they might have gone this way."

The woman's stare turned into a glare. "Was the alarm ringing BEFORE you opened the door to run down here?" she asked.

"Oh..." said Sally. "No." She looked at her **_DETECTIVE_** partner. "_We_ must have set the alarm off when we opened the door!"

"Oh," said Fetch. **_WOOF!_**

GENERAL MANAGER Claire walked back down to a bend in the stairs. On the wall was a small electronic box. She pulled a key card out of her pocket and touched it against the box. The alarm stopped.

The silence that followed was so silent that, if you drew it, it would be a big, black hole.

A small, yellow square of paper had fallen from **_GENERAL MANAGER_** Claire's pocket when she'd pulled out her key card: a sticky note. Sally bent down, picked it up and handed it back to her.

"Thank you," said Claire.

CAPTAIN BOFF

The top lawn
Friday 3 p.m.

Sally managed to read the note before handing it over.

"Follow me," said Claire, sounding friendlier now. "You can come out through reception then go back up in the lift.

You have a very handsome dog, I must say. What's its name?"

"He's a *he*, not an *it*, General," Sally explained. "His name is Fetch. We're **DETECTIVES**."

"Really?"

WOOF! agreed Fetch.

"Tell me about the shampoo-and-clean-towel **thieves**," said Claire.

"It'll be in our **report**, General," said **DETECTIVE** Sally Stick, "when we **solve** it."

Claire smiled at the pair. "By the way," she began, "I'm not a Gen—" But the **DETECTIVES** had gone.

✳

Stick and Fetch decided it would be a
sensible idea to get back to Room 402
as soon as possible, especially if Granny
Stick had heard the alarm.

Fetch managed to tread on one
of his own ears and do an accidental
somersault, while trying to run and talk to
Sally at the same time. He yapped.

An elderly man in a Navy uniform stuck his head out of Room 422. "What's going on?" he asked. "What was that alarm and why's that dog barking?"

"There's nothing to worry about, sir," said Sally Stick in her best **DETECTIVE** voice. "We have everything under control."

"You do?" asked the old man, raising a very white eyebrow in surprise.

Sally lowered her voice and leant towards the man. "I probably shouldn't be telling you this, sir, because we're working **undercover**, but –" she pointed at her wet-nosed, waggy-tailed, tongue-lolling partner – "Fetch and I are **DETECTIVES**."

"Really?" said the old man, with a twinkle in his eye. "Aren't you a little young to be a **DETECTIVE**, Miss – er...?"

"Stick," said Sally. "Sally Stick. And looking like an ordinary girl with an ordinary dog is a very useful disguise."

"Ordinary?" said Fetch indignantly.

Sally dropped to her knees and rubbed Fetch's ears. "OF COURSE, I don't think you're ordinary," she said. "I think you're the most extra-special, handsome, EXTRAORDINARY dog there is... But, because you're such a good **DETECTIVE**, you can disguise yourself as ordinary."

Fetch gave Sally some extra-special licks on the face.

"Well, good luck to you both," said the elderly man. He had a very smiley face.

Sally Stick took her **DETECTIVE** notepad and **DETECTIVE** pencil out of her top pocket. "Could I take your name, please, sir?" she said. "It's for my **report**."

"My name?" said the man. "For your **report**? Why, certainly, **DETECTIVE**! It's Captain Boff." He spelled out B-O-F-F for her, which was very helpful.

"Nice to meet you, Captain," said Sally,

Captain BOFF

putting away the notebook and pencil. "It's exciting to meet a real live soldier."

"I'm an old sea dog, not a soldier," the man explained. "Nice to meet you two, too. Goodbye!" He closed the door to his hotel room.

"He's not a dog!" said a puzzled Fetch.

"He means a sailor, Fetch!" said Sally, giving him a loving stroke. "There are salty sea dogs in my **pirate book**!"

Fetch had stopped listening. "Did you see that?" **WOOF!**

"See what?"

"The captain has a CAT in his room! I saw it behind him, through the gap in the doorway."

"This is a pet-friendly hotel," Sally reminded him. "He's allowed to have a cat."

"The cat was wearing a cap."

"What?"

"His cat was wearing a sailor's cap!"

"Perhaps the captain has a spare."

"But it was a cat-sized cap..." said Fetch.

"Hmmm," said Sally Stick. "Now that IS strange! And it was the captain's name on the note **_GENERAL MANAGER_** Claire dropped. Staying at this hotel is getting more and more interesting!"

CHAPTER 4

AN UNINVITED VISITOR

STICK & FETCH found Granny Stick back in the room. She had changed her clothes and done her hair. "It was only a short nap but I feel refreshed," she said. "What have you two been up to?"

"Oh, this and that," said Sally innocently.

"Any **DETECTING**?"

"You bet!" said Fetch. **WOOF!**

"Maybe a little," said Sally.

"Let's go down for supper," said Granny.

Fetch had to stay up in the room because animals weren't allowed in the hotel restaurant. He dived under Sally's bed, picked up Squeaky Duck in his mouth then backed out again, bottom wiggling

wag

wiggle
wiggle

and tail wagging. He jumped into his bed
and snuggled down with Squeaky Duck
between his paws.

"I think I'll have a little snooze," he
woofed.

"Fetch says he's going to have a
snooze," Sally told Granny Stick.

"Now there's a surprise!" said Granny.

Sally felt very grown-up eating in
The Roxbee Hotel restaurant.
The tables were covered in thick white
linen cloths, and the silver knives and
forks had heavy swirly-patterned handles.
The waitress even put a napkin on Sally's
lap for her!

To start with, Sally had carrot and
coriander soup with a nice warm crusty
roll on a little side plate.

For her main course Sally  had a

beanburger

with thick-cut chips

made from sweet potatoes,

and some VERY shiny green beans.

Granny Stick had something called a

five-bean salad.

"I can see more than five beans in it,

Granny!" said Sally when it arrived.

"You're right!" Granny Stick laughed. "It's called a five-bean salad because it has five DIFFERENT types of bean in it."

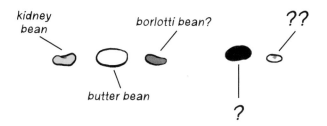

kidney bean

borlotti bean?

??

butter bean

?

"This red one is definitely a kidney bean," said Granny Stick. "And this is a butter bean ... and I *think* this is called a borlotti bean... But I'm not sure about these two." She prodded a white and a black bean. "We'll ask the waitress when she comes back."

The waitress had no idea either, so she said she'd ask the chef.

Sally was eating vanilla ice cream with chocolate sauce from a little silver bowl, and Granny Stick was sipping coffee from a tiny gold-coloured china cup, when a man appeared beside their table. He was wearing a tall, thin chef's hat and black-and-white checked trousers, which made Sally Stick's eyes zing.

"Good evening, ladies!" he said, with a smile. "I hope you have enjoyed your meal."

"Very much," said Granny Stick.

"Yes, thank you," said Sally.

"I believe you were asking which five beans go in the five-bean salad?"

"Yes," said Granny Stick. "I recognized three of them, but—"

She was about to say more when she was interrupted by a very familiar **WOOF!** and some startled cries from diners at other tables.

"Fetch!" cried Sally. For it was her **DETECTIVE** partner, of course. "What is it?"

A rather wet Fetch came bounding between the tables, panting loudly.

"No pets in the restaurant!" shouted the horrified chef.

So what had happened to make Fetch run down to the restaurant? And why was he so wet? Well, if you remember, Sally and Granny Stick had left Fetch curled up with Squeaky Duck in his own bed, but he'd soon moved on to Sally's. After a while, he woke up with the strangest feeling that he wasn't alone...

Fetch jumped down and ran into the other room. There was a man at the window! Granny Stick had left the window open to let some air in, and the man looked as if he was about to open it wider.

Fetch stared at him. The man was wearing a black-and-white striped top.

*Don't **burglars** usually wear black-and-white striped tops?* Fetch thought.

Although Fetch is quite a SMALL dog, he's a **DETECTIVE** dog and a very brave one, at that. He knew that he must guard the room. It had important things in it like Sally's Scruff and his Squeaky Duck and Granny's favourite seashell necklace. And, of course, there were little shampoo bottles and clean towels, too!

*That's what the **burglar** must be after,* he thought.

And with that, Fetch jumped at the man through the gap in the bottom of the window.

Fetch had never seen anyone climb down a ladder so fast! The truth be told, he'd seen very few people climb down ladders at any speed, except for Mr Tamsin, Granny Stick's next-door-but-one neighbour, who comes and cleans her windows every once in a while.

The man was holding a bucket, which Fetch landed in with a **SPLASH!**

Much to Fetch's relief, the man didn't drop the bucket — or him — until they reached the ground. There, the bucket was abandoned and the man ran away.

A soggy Fetch leapt out of the bucket and ran, barking, after him.

WOOF! "And don't come back!"

Job done, Fetch bounded around to the front of the hotel, his paws sending gravel flying, and dashed up the steps, through the main entrance and into reception.

From there, he made straight for the restaurant and his **DETECTIVE** partner … only to be stopped by the chef.

"It's the water in the bucket that makes no sense," said Sally later when she'd had her **DETECTIVE** partner's full **report** of the incident. Fetch put on his thinking cap. Actually, it was a towel. "I know!" said Sally. "If a **burglar** dropped those little shampoo bottles into a bucket they would make a clattering noise and might attract attention..."

WOOF! agreed Fetch, leaping up and down, excitedly.

"So," said Sally Stick, "dropping them in water would muffle the sound!"

"Those dastardly **thieves** thought of everything!" growled Fetch. **GRRRRRRRR.**

"Not everything, Fetch," said Sally, proudly. "They didn't think that YOU'D be there to save the day!"

CHAPTER 5

CAPTAIN BOFF

he next few days passed quickly, with big exciting breakfasts where Sally could help herself to cereal, yogurts, fruit salad, orange juice, croissants, cheese, pains au chocolat and a whole host of other things from a counter. A waiter would bring Granny some coffee and Sally a mug of hot chocolate to their table.

They could also order a cooked breakfast off a menu. Sally was usually full by then, but she always ordered some sausages, which she then rolled up in her napkin and took to their room to give to Fetch. After all, it was *his* holiday too.

The Sticks made plenty of trips to the beach. Granny Stick liked to sit and read and guard the picnic while Sally and Fetch liked to paddle in the sea. Fetch liked it best when he was in deep enough water for his ears to float on the surface.

Once, when they made sandcastles,
Granny Stick produced some tiny flags on
wooden toothpick flagpoles to go on top.

One day on the beach, Stick and Fetch
helped a boy called Alf solve the *mystery*
of his missing spade. His little sisters had
buried it in the sand. **DETECTIVE** Fetch's

super-sensitive doggie nose came in VERY handy that time.

On another occasion, Granny Stick **solved** the *mystery* of the two disappearing ice lollies. She guessed that Sally and Fetch had eaten them!

Stick and Fetch thought it was funny that Granny Stick liked to play at being a **DETECTIVE** while they were real ones.

Sally Stick had started wearing sunglasses, sometimes. "It's for two reasons," she told Fetch. "Firstly, so that people don't recognize me."

"We are famous **DETECTIVES**, after all," Fetch agreed. **WOOF!**

"And secondly, so that no one can see that I'm keeping an eye on things."

This made Fetch want to wear sunglasses too, so Sally bought him a pair with her holiday money. When she put them on him, he felt even more **DETECTIVE-Y**!

STICK & FETCH are very rarely off duty, but they were SO busy doing holiday things that they almost forgot they were on a case.

Then, on the last afternoon, Granny Stick went up to Room 402 for a nap. "All this lovely sunshine makes me tired," she said. She left Fetch and Sally playing in the hotel gardens under the watchful eye of the hotel entertainment manager.

The gardens were huge with several lawns and large trees. Fetch likes trees! He and Sally – along with other dogs and their owners – were running around a doggie obstacle course, which had been

set up in an area near
the car park.

Then something caught
Sally's eye. "Look at that!"
she said. She pointed at a
canvas gazebo, which had
just been put up on one of
the lawns. A white-haired
man with a great big
beard, and wearing a
peaked cap, was

RUMBLE
UNION

114

sitting under it. "It's Captain Boff!"

Fetch was more interested in the cat
sitting very still on the chair next to the
captain: it was the one he'd caught a
glimpse of in the captain's room; the one
wearing its own little cat-sized captain's
cap!

Fetch sniffed the air with his super-sensitive **DETECTIVE**-trained doggy nose.

That's odd! he thought.

He couldn't smell the horrid cat. But he could smell shampoo. It was the smell of shampoo from those little bottles... The

little bottles that the shampoo-and-clean-towel **thieves** had on their **GETAWAY TROLLEY**! And it was a very STRONG smell.

Stick and Fetch had forgotten all about the doggie obstacle course. They were back on the case, keeping a professional eye on the captain and his most unusual moggy.

Fetch growled as he told Sally what he could smell.

"There's something fishy about Captain Boff," agreed Sally. "Even if he doesn't smell fishy but of *STOLEN* SHAMPOO!"

"Actually," said Fetch, "I think that's the cat."

Sally Stick suddenly got VERY excited. "Maybe the captain has trained the cat to *STEAL* the shampoos for him while he takes the clean towels! Maybe he's a cat **burglar**!"

Captain Boff had spotted them.

"Ah, the *DETECTIVE* duo!" he called out, his face breaking into a smile. "Want to meet my old crew?"

Sally realized that she and Fetch had been so busy trying to get a good close look at the captain's cat, they'd ignored

a group of elderly men who'd spilled out of a minibus. Dressed in old Navy uniforms, they were now crossing the lawn, some waving. Captain Boff turned to greet them.

"Maybe later, Captain!" Sally shouted.

"Follow me," she whispered to Fetch.

Stick and Fetch sat themselves on a bench beneath a huge oak tree, out of sight.

"We need to look at the facts again," said Sally.

WOOF! said Stick (which simply meant "**WOOF!**" in this instance).

Sally took her **DETECTIVE** notebook
from her pocket and read aloud from it.

1. There was a **TROLLEY** with *STOLEN*
   shampoos and clean towels on it.
2. There was a cupboard where one of
   the **villains** hid and ate a 𝔹𝔸ℕ𝔻𝕀𝕋 bar.
3. The **villains** can't have used the back
   stairs to escape (because we set the
   alarm off, not them).

"Are you with me so far?"

"Yes," panted Fetch.

"Then we saw the captain at his door—"

"And the cat in a captain's cap behind him!" added Fetch. He spat out the word cat like a cat spits out a furball.

"But what if he wasn't opening his door to see what all the noise was about? What if he was going back INTO his room and only pretending to be coming out?"

"YES!" Fetch gasped.

"And we went and told him that we're **DETECTIVES**!" said Sally, the cogs in her **DETECTIVE**'s brain spinning and whirring as she tried to make sense of it all. "And the next thing we know, someone's trying to climb in through our window at supper time!"

WOOF! Fetch was so excited that his ears were misbehaving.

"The captain could have sent one of his **CRIMINAL GANG** to our room, not to **STEAL** but to search the room for documents to see how much we know!" said Sally Stick. "It's lucky I always keep my notes with me." She patted her **DETECTIVE** notebook, which she'd just put back in the front pocket of her dress.

Fetch wanted to talk about the cat that didn't smell of cat but of shampoo.

"No real live cat would let you shampoo it!" said Sally Stick. "You're a genius, Fetch! It's obviously a STUFFED CAT!"

Fetch didn't see what a stuffed cat had to do with the **thefts**. He scratched behind his ear with a back leg.

scratch
scratch

"Once the captain knew that two top **DETECTIVES** were staying at the hotel, maybe he wanted to distract us from the case. Top **villains** like him probably do background research ... and he must have found out that you hate cats!"

"Or ..." said Fetch, quivering with excitement, "... maybe the stuffed cat is stuffed full of *STOLEN* shampoo bottles. That's how they're going to smuggle them out!"

DETECTIVE Sally Stick lifted Fetch into the air and kissed his nose. "You, partner, are a GENIUS!" she said. "We should soon be in a position to make **arrests**."

CHAPTER 6

JUSTICE AT LAST!

A few minutes later, **GENERAL MANAGER** Claire came into the garden through the big French windows. She stepped around the foot of a ladder belonging to a member of hotel staff who was busy cleaning an upstairs window. She strode out across the lawn.

"Hello, you two!" She greeted Stick and Fetch with a friendly smile.

"Hello, **GENERAL**!" said Sally, smiling sweetly back.

Claire looked at her watch. "Hmm. Five to three," she said to herself. Then, to the two **DETECTIVES**," she said, "I'd better get a move on!" And off she went.

When she was out of earshot, Sally hissed excitedly to Fetch, "Five minutes to three! Three o'clock was the time written on the sticky note the **GENERAL** dropped!

CAPTAIN BOFF

The top lawn
Friday 3 p.m.

It's Friday today, and now she's heading straight for Captain Boff. Something big is going to happen!"

Fetch growled. He was ready for action!

"But why is *The Roxbee*'s **GENERAL MANAGER** meeting up with a shampoo-and-clean-towel **thief**?" Sally wondered. "These **thefts** must be an inside job!"

Fetch gave a doggie frown. "But they're

both *outside*," he protested.

"I mean that someone working inside the hotel is also working with the shampoo-and-clean-towel **thieves**!" said Sally.

"WOW!" said her doggy **DETECTIVE** partner. **WOOF!**

"It's time we, er..." Sally was trying to remember a phrase from her **BIG BOOK OF DETECTIVE TALES**. According to the book, there were two common ways to unmask the **culprit**:

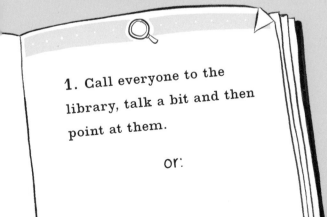

1. Call everyone to the library, talk a bit and then point at them.

or:

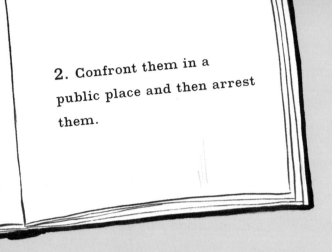

2. Confront them in a public place and then arrest them.

The library approach isn't very practical for STICK & FETCH. It's very difficult for a girl and her dog — even if they are *very* good **DETECTIVES** — to get grown-ups to gather anywhere so that one of them can be unmasked as a **culprit.***

*Except for one time when the **culprits** were actually IN their local library.

This is why **STICK & FETCH** nearly always go for the second one.

"Confront them in a public space!" said Sally, remembering the phrase just in time. She stood up. "Come on, partner!"

WOOF!

"You mean we tackle Captain Boff, the cat in the cap and Claire the ***GENERAL-MANAGER-WHO-ISN'T-REALLY-A-GENERAL*** all at once?" Fetch barked.

"Yes," said Sally Stick. "That's exactly what I'm suggesting!"

When the pair came out from under the tree, Captain Boff and his old ship's crew were sitting in the gazebo listening to **GENERAL MANAGER** Claire. She was making a speech: "It's such an honour for *The Roxbee Hotel* to be chosen for such an important reunion. How wonderful to have so many of you here, including your old mascot Baggy, the ship's cat—"

It was time for STICK & FETCH,
DETECTIVES to confront the international
GANG of small-hotel-bottles-of-shampoo-
and-clean-towel **thieves** in public!

"Let's make some **arrests**!" cried
Sally Stick. The pair of them CHARGED.

Three other dogs, who'd been doing the doggy assault course, saw that Fetch was allowed off the leash to play with the captain and decided to join in!

Children laughed and cheered while the grown-ups tried to call their dogs back. There was plenty of whistling and "Bad dog!" and "Here, boy!" and "Good girl!" and barking and yelping and – here's a brilliant word – it was PANDEMONIUM.

Fetch's first target was Baggy, the cat in the captain's cap. After all, a cat is a cat whether it's alive or stuffed with bottles of shampoo.

He sank his teeth into its tail.

"Did you enjoy your stay at *The Roxbee Hotel*?" asked Granny Stick the following morning as they stood in reception with their luggage.

"Oh, yes!" said Sally Stick.

"Yes!" barked Fetch. **WOOF!**

"We had a lovely time, thank you, Granny," said Sally. "Best holiday EVER!"

"It's such a shame that something spooked all the dogs on the doggie assault course yesterday," said Granny Stick. "It sounds like it was mayhem out there."

"It didn't spoil things one bit, Granny!" Sally assured her.

Morris appeared at their side and picked up their luggage. Just then, a taxi pulled up in the driveway.

"We even got to **solve** a case," added Sally.

"An important case," Fetch said.

"You **solved** a case?" asked Granny Stick as they did up their seat belts in the taxi. "I am pleased. I didn't think you'd find any *mysteries* to **solve** in a quiet hotel."

Sally Stick picked up Fetch to carry him into the car. He licked her on the nose.

If only Granny knew!

Sally smiled. She was already looking forward to the next case for STICK & FETCH, DETECTIVES.

THE END

PHILIP ARDAGH has won lots of awards, mostly for writing. Not one is for detecting. He's never had a dog, but if he did, he'd want one just like Fetch. Philip does have a big bushy beard, though, and they go everywhere together.

ELISSA ELWICK writes as well as illustrates, but, like Philip, never quite got the knack of detecting. She grew up with dogs around the house and hopes to have a real-life Fetch of her own one day. She recently got a cat called Pippin, and she's not sure Fetch has quite forgiven her yet...